Can you keep a secret? You can? GOOD.

This book will share with you the secrets of some special little animals called teezles who are so clever they could almost be called magic.

These happy little creatures live in Crabapple Wood, where they build their underground homes beneath large trees. They get their surnames from the tree under which they live.

They live in peace with all other animals, insects and birds and help them when they are injured, sick or in need.

Although teezles use nature's gifts in many wonderful ways, they always protect and preserve the countryside.

So! If you are good and kind and always care for the wonderful things that life gives to us then, maybe one day, you could become a friend of the teezles.

"GO JOYFULLY" THROUGH LIFE

THE TEEZLES and the SNOW RABBIT

by Terry Barber

Published by Peter Haddock Limited,
Bridlington, England.

© Terry Barber

Illustrated by Wizard Art,
courtesy of Bernard Thornton Artists, London.

THE TEEZLES and the SNOW RABBIT

Winter had come to Crabapple Wood and the teezles knew that a blizzard was on the way. The wood was strangely quiet. Cosy Beech and her husband, Linden, were hurriedly gathering the last few nuts and acorns off the ground before the snow came. Suddenly, a piercing scream shattered the silence. "What on earth was that?" exclaimed Cosy. "Sounds like an animal in pain," answered Linden as they hurried off to investigate.

Soon a pitiful sight met their eyes. A beautiful white rabbit lay trapped in a snare. The wire loop of the man animal trap had tightened around her back leg and, as the terrified animal tried to pull away, the wire cut further into her flesh, causing it to bleed very badly.

"Don't move," said Linden firmly but gently. The young rabbit lay still, moaning and shivering with shock. Cosy and Linden gently lifted her and eased the wire loop off her leg. The rabbit tried to get up, but cried out in pain and collapsed again. "She is too badly injured to walk. You go and get help and I will stay with her," said Cosy. Linden hurried off.

When Linden returned with the other teezles the snow was beginning to fall.

"We must find a sheltered place to tend her wound," said Silk. "I know just the spot," exclaimed Lark Holly. "It's near your oak tree. I will go and prepare it."

As Lark ran off, they lifted the rabbit on to a large piece of bark, which acted as a stretcher, and followed him through the thickening snow.

Lark had prepared a bed of dry straw inside a hollow tree trunk. They carried the rabbit inside and gently laid her down.

"This is ideal," said Silk, as she began to tend the wound. But the rabbit screamed out in pain. Silk took a bottle from her basket and poured out a spoonful of soothing medicine for her. Soon the rabbit was in a deep sleep and Silk was able to dress the wound.

Silk and Fragrance decided to stay with the rabbit. Lark and Linden covered the entrance with bark and ferns to keep out the snow and wind. Fern brought heating rings, which teezles use for heating and cooking, and bright wax lanterns to light the temporary sick bay. Cosy brought food for them all.

For two days and nights the blizzard raged. As the rabbit gradually regained her strength, she told them that her name was Snowy and that she was the pet of a man animal family who lived in a cottage at the edge of a wood. The child of the family, who was called Mary, had left the door of the hutch open and the rabbit had decided to have an adventure. She wandered into the wood and into the cruel trap.

"Well, let's hope you enjoy your freedom," said Fragrance, as Fern popped his head through the opening.

"You can come out. The storm is over," he said.

Teezles love playing in snow and Snowy played happily with them. At first her leg was sore and stiff, but within a few days she didn't even limp.

They slid down the hills on laurel leaves and had snowball fights. Snowy flicked snow into their faces with her back legs.

Clumsy Tub started to make a giant snowball but he got caught up in it and rolled down the hill, knocking over other teezles on the way.

Everyone loved Snowy and one morning she awoke to find a massive rabbit made of snow. The teezles had worked all night to surprise her.

As the days passed the teezles began to notice that Snowy looked very sad and one morning Linden found her crying. "What is the matter?" he asked gently. "You have all been so kind and I love you dearly, but I miss Mary and her family and I want to go home." "So you shall," said Linden.

The snow had nearly melted as the teezles escorted Snowy to the edge of the wood. "Goodbye, I shall miss you all," said Snowy tearfully. Silk kissed the rabbit tenderly. "Be happy and Go Joyfully," she whispered.

FAMILY QUESTION

What is the difference between a rabbit and a hare?

If you don't know, go to your local library and look for a book to help you find out.

The rabbit scampered down the hill to the cottage. Mary was playing in the garden. When she saw Snowy she screamed with delight.

"Mummy, Daddy, Snowy has come home," she cried, picking up the rabbit and hugging her. Mary's parents appeared at the door.

"Where have you been and what have you been up to?" asked the father. Of course, the rabbit could not tell him, but we could, couldn't we?

FAMILY
QUEST

See how many evergreen trees and plants you can find and identify.